Translation copyright © 2008 by Rabén & Sjögren Bokförlag
All rights reserved
Originally published in Sweden by Rabén & Sjögren under the title *Ellens äppelträd*
Copyright © 2006 by Catarina Kruusval
Library of Congress Control Number: 2007939441
Printed in Denmark
First American edition, 2008
ISBN-13: 978-91-29-66905-3
ISBN-10: 91-29-66905-7

*Rabén & Sjögren Bokförlag is part of
Norstedts Publishing Group, established in 1823*

Catarina Kruusval

Ellen's APPLE TREE

Translated by Joan Sandin

R&S
BOOKS

Stockholm New York London Adelaide Toronto

Ellen lives in a house with a yard
all around it. It's a small yard
with neat little flower beds
where no one is allowed
to walk.

But there are other places Ellen can go—in the playhouse that Papa built or in the sandbox, also built by Papa, or on the big rock that is Ellen's Small Mountain.

In the middle of the yard is a big apple tree. That's where Ellen likes to be most of all.

So does Ollie. Ollie is Ellen's friend. Both of them like to climb in the apple tree.

In the spring, when all the flowers are in bloom, the apple tree looks completely white.

Ellen and Ollie each have their very own sitting branch. Ellen's branch is higher up in the tree than Ollie's. They can sit up there and peek out through all the whiteness.

In the summer, the tree is like a green cave. When they sit inside, they can see everything happening down on the ground. But no one can see them sitting up there watching.

"Our secret place," says Ellen.

"I'm a spy," says Ollie.

"Me, too," says Ellen. "An apple tree spy." Then she takes a bite out of an apple. It's green and hard and doesn't taste very good.

"Not ripe yet," she says, and spits it out.

In the fall, the little green apples turn into yellow and red apples, and then they taste good. Ellen and Ollie climb around in the tree, picking all the apples they can reach. Ellen's mama and papa put some of the apples in boxes.

"We'll save these for later in the fall," they say. Some of the apples drop by themselves, bouncing down on the grass, or on someone's head if they're not watching out.

"Windfalls," says Ellen's papa, putting those apples in plastic bags.

Ellen's mama sets one of the bags out by the gate.

Windfall apples for the horses

It isn't very long before the chilly weather
begins. Flowers and leaves dry up and the sky is mostly gray.
One day, it starts to snow. Big white snowflakes float down.
    Ellen and Ollie play outside in the snow all day. When they
come in, they sit by the kitchen window, eating applesauce and
drinking milk. Outside, snowflakes are swirling around. The wind
begins to blow a little, making the branches on the apple tree sway
back and forth.

By evening, the wind is blowing so hard it makes a crackling noise.

"The wind is picking up," says Ellen's papa when he comes inside. "I'm thinking we might get a storm."

"Do you think the house will hold together?" asks Ellen's mama, worried.

"Yes," he answers. "But I'm not so sure about the electricity." Just then the whole house goes dark.

"Oh no!" he says. They fumble around in pitch black, searching for flashlights and candles.

The radiators become ice cold, and everybody has to wear sweaters and jackets inside the house. Ellen's papa makes a fire in the fireplace, and at bedtime they get their blankets and pillows and settle in on the floor in front of the fire.

They lie there listening to the storm, still whistling outside. Mama and Papa are worried, but Ellen thinks it's nice lying in front of the fire, all three of them close together.

"This is how I want it to be all the time," she whispers into the darkness.

The next morning, the wind has stopped blowing. The radiators are warm again and the lights are back on. Ollie knocks on the door.

"Did you see what happened," he says, pointing outside, "to THE APPLE TREE!!"

The entire tree is lying in the snow, a messy heap of branches and twigs. Only the broken-off trunk is sticking up out of the snow. The storm has taken down their wonderful big apple tree. They go outside and Ellen's papa follows them.

"What a shame," he says. "It was such a splendid apple tree." He goes to get a saw while Ellen and Ollie climb around in the fallen branches.

"This is probably my branch," says Ollie, sitting down on it.

"I can't find mine," says Ellen. She sits down beside him.

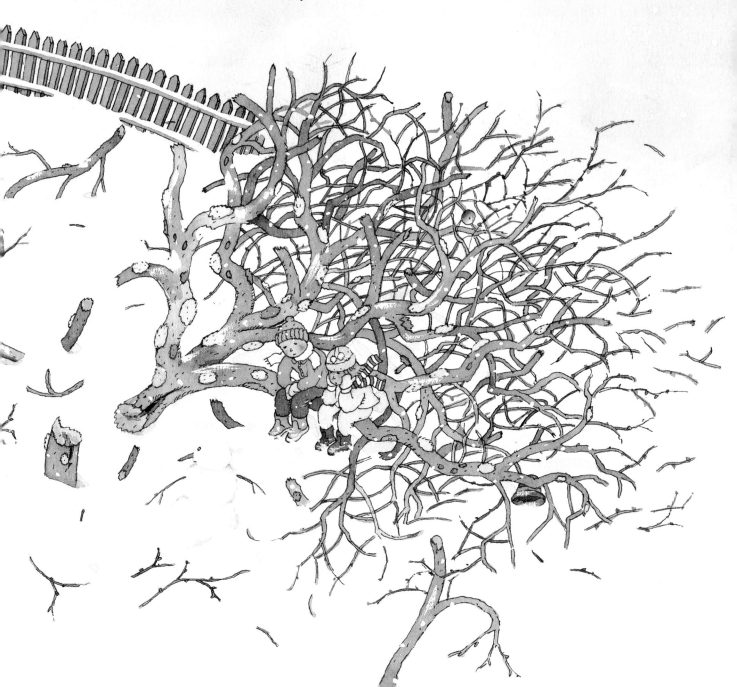

Every day they talk about the apple tree, about how wonderful it was. Ellen's mama frames a picture of the tree and hangs it in the hallway.

Now Ellen and Ollie have to find other places to play in the yard. Of course, they still have Ellen's Small Mountain and the playhouse. Because it's winter and there's snow on the ground, they can build snowmen and igloos, throw snowballs, and do other winter things. Sometimes they even forget that an apple tree once stood in the yard, where there's now an empty space.

One day, Ellen's mama takes out two apples.

"These are the last ones," she says, giving one to Ellen and one to Ollie. "Now all the apples from our tree are gone."

Ellen and Ollie look at the apples. Neither of them wants to bite into the LAST apple.

"I'm going to save mine," says Ellen. "I don't want them to be gone. I'm going to keep my apple FOREVER!"

"You know what?" says Mama. "We'll get a new tree in the spring. We'll buy one just like the old tree."

"YES!" cry Ellen and Ollie.

Ellen and Ollie wait impatiently
for spring to come.

"Today is spring," they say
right after Christmas.

"No," says Ellen's papa,
brushing off some snow.
"Today is not spring."

"Well, today it must be spring,"
they say one day when it
suddenly starts raining, making
the snow all wet and slushy.

"No, not yet," says Ellen's
papa.

"But TODAY," says Ellen's
mama when the first
snowdrops begin sticking
up through the snow,
"today spring is
STARTING anyway."

Finally, spring really comes. The sun is shining every day, and they can go outside with only a sweater on.

Ellen's mama gets a shovel and starts digging a big hole in the yard. She works hard to dig out the root of the old apple tree. But it's not until Ellen's papa gets a crowbar that they are able to loosen the root and lift it out of the hole.

"Well, there certainly wasn't anything wrong with the root," Ellen's mama says. "No storm in the world could have gotten to it."

The next day they go to the garden center, where there are lots of trees. They walk around reading the labels.

"Ingrid Marie, Cox Orange . . ." Mama reads. "What kind of apple tree did we have?"

"Well, it couldn't have been any of these," says Ellen.

"Really?" says her mama. "Do you know what kind it was?"

"I do," says Ellen, and shows her.

"It was a BIG tree. Much bigger than these itty-bitty things."

Ellen's mama laughs. "Every tree is this small in the beginning," she says. "It takes years before they become as big as ours was. We can't buy a tree as big as that one."

Ellen is quiet. She looks over at Ollie. This is disappointing news.

"How long will it take before we can climb in it?" asks Ollie.

Ellen's mama thinks a minute.

"Maybe nine or ten years," she says, poking around in the skinny little trees.

"Look!" she says suddenly. "This is it! Golden Red. It has to be the tree." And she brings it to the checkout counter.

"I feel sorry for this tree," says Ellen. "It's so little."

When they get home, they plant the tree together. Then they stand back and look at the stick in the ground that's supposed to be their new apple tree.

"It will get some leaves soon," says Ollie. "Then it will look better."

And he's right! After a week, some small light-green leaves are sticking out on the branches.

"Look!" says Ollie. "I think there are flowers, too!"

"And here comes a bee!" shouts Ellen.

The small green leaves turn into [leaves, and new branches grow o] the trunk. Soon the little tree look[real tree.

When fall comes, it's harvest time—just ONE big apple.

They cut it up into four pieces.

One piece is for Ellen's mama, one for her papa, one for Ollie, and one for Ellen.

"An unusually good apple," says Ellen's papa,
smacking his lips. Everybody agrees.
"An unusually good little tree," says Ellen.
And they all agree on that as well.